RUPERT

CAN

DANCE

Jules Feiffer

Michael di Capua Books • Farrar Straus Giroux

For Lily

Printed in China by South China Printing
Library of Congress control number: 2013908976
Designed by Steve Scott • First edition, 2014

Rupert . . .

loved to watch Mandy dance.

Day and night, Rupert watched Mandy.

The only time she stopped dancing
was when she went to sleep at night.

Don't worry, Rupert,
I'll dance some more when
I wake up tomorrow.

No more than a minute or two
after Mandy was asleep

Rupert tiptoed over to her closet

and slipped on her dancing shoes.

Now it was Rupert's turn to dance,
As Mandy slept the night away

Rupert danced the night away.

You can *not* believe how good he was.

Not just a good dancer,
but also a quiet dancer.

Dancing was Rupert's secret!

And the last thing he wanted
was for Mandy to wake up and find out.

Rupert loved having a secret from Mandy.
Cats love secrets

and Rupert took great pride
that his secret was one of the best ever.

Then one night Mandy woke up
when she wasn't supposed to.

Rupert!
You're
dancing!

Rupert was caught flat-footed.
His secret was out!

Immediately, he jumped out of
Mandy's dancing shoes.

And he fled under her bed.

Rupert,
I didn't know you
could dance!

This was the very thing Rupert wanted to avoid.

Mandy was giving him dancing lessons!

Rupert was mortified. The fun in dancing
was to do it his own way. In secret.
And without having to take lessons.

Dogs might qualify for lessons, but Rupert was a cat.

Cats are not meant for lessons. Cats are free spirits.

Rupert lost all interest in ever dancing again.

Poor Mandy!

She couldn't understand why her cat
was spending all his time under the bed.

At school, when she should have been thinking
about math and science . . .

she was thinking about Rupert.

Three days after he went into hiding,
Mandy came up with an idea.

The idea led to a plan.

She put her plan into action.

What?

Was Mandy actually asking Rupert for help?

Slowly . . .

Rupert crawled out from under the bed.

Slowly . . .

he headed straight for Mandy's closet.

He thought Mandy might need her dancing shoes,
so Rupert slipped into her sneakers.

And he danced.

Oh . . .
I see.

Now I get it.

Yes, for the first time since his secret
was revealed, Rupert danced.

They could have gone on this way

for years.

And in fact

they did.